EGGBERT

The Slightly Cracked Egg

BY **TOM ROSS**

ILLUSTRATED BY **REX BARRON**

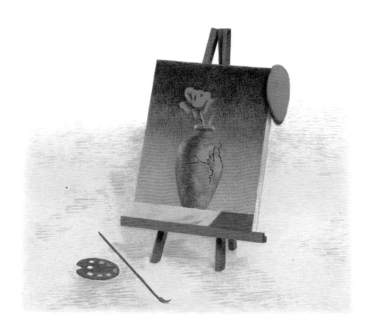

The Putnam & Grosset Group

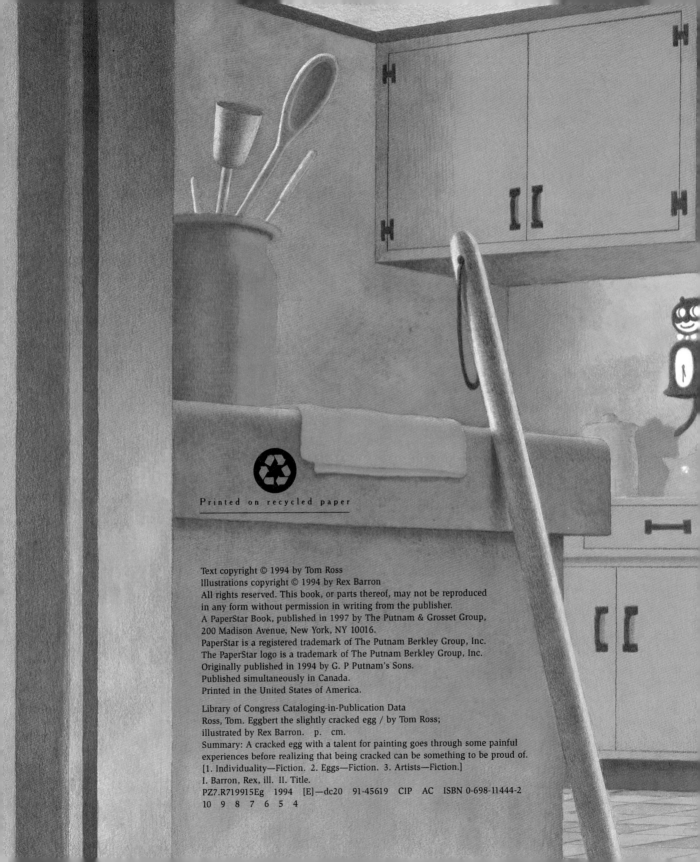

Text copyright © 1994 by Tom Ross
Illustrations copyright © 1994 by Rex Barron
All rights reserved. This book, or parts thereof, may not be reproduced
in any form without permission in writing from the publisher.
A PaperStar Book, published in 1997 by The Putnam & Grosset Group,
200 Madison Avenue, New York, NY 10016.
PaperStar is a registered trademark of The Putnam Berkley Group, Inc.
The PaperStar logo is a trademark of The Putnam Berkley Group, Inc.
Originally published in 1994 by G. P Putnam's Sons.
Published simultaneously in Canada.
Printed in the United States of America.

Library of Congress Cataloging-in-Publication Data
Ross, Tom. Eggbert the slightly cracked egg / by Tom Ross;
illustrated by Rex Barron.   p.   cm.
Summary: A cracked egg with a talent for painting goes through some painful
experiences before realizing that being cracked can be something to be proud of.
[1. Individuality—Fiction. 2. Eggs—Fiction. 3. Artists—Fiction.]
I. Barron, Rex, ill. II. Title.
PZ7.R719915Eg 1994 [E]—dc20 91-45619 CIP AC ISBN 0-698-11444-2
10 9 8 7 6 5 4

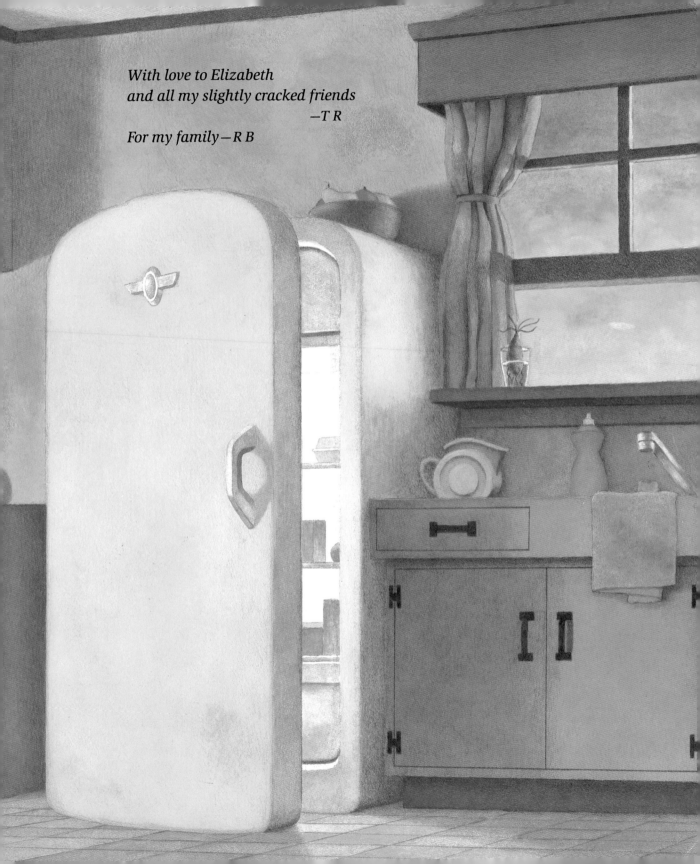

There once was an egg named Eggbert. He loved to paint beautiful pictures.

Eggbert's paintings always cheered up the other eggs in the refrigerator.

But one day it was discovered that Eggbert was slightly cracked.

Eggs with cracked shells were not allowed to stay.
Sadly, the other eggs told Eggbert he would have
to leave.

Eggbert waved good-bye to his old friends. He hunched his shoulders — what little shoulders he had — and pressed his shell together, so that the crack almost disappeared.

Almost.

CRISPER

Then he set out to look for a new place to live. All the drawers had labels, but none of them was right for Eggbert. He knew he would have to look harder. There had to be *some* place where he would fit in.

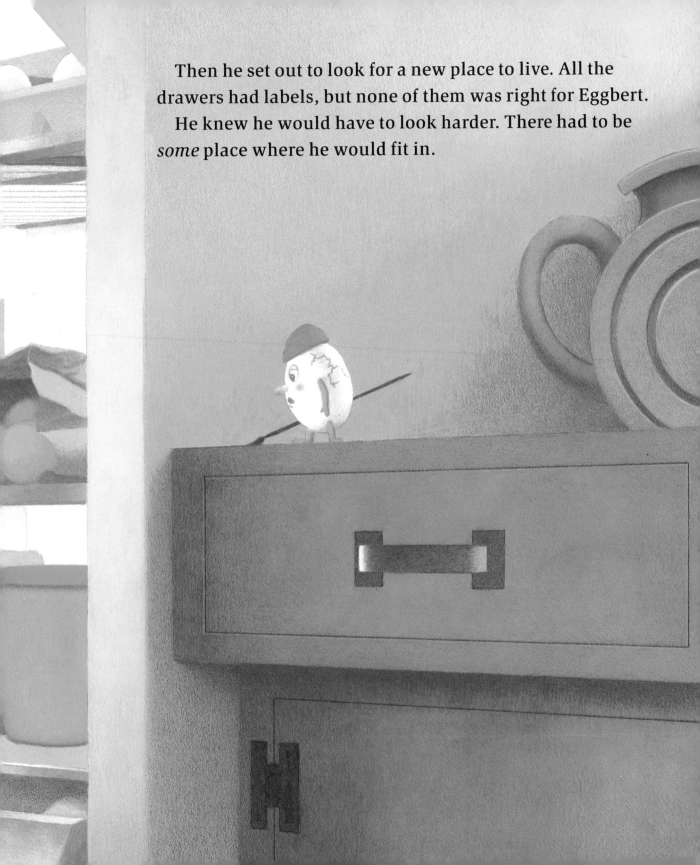

Before long Eggbert came to a spot with a beautiful view. If only I could stay here, he thought. Then he had a great idea.

No one had to know that he was an egg with a cracked shell. He would paint himself to look like the other things around him. He'd blend right in.

But just as Eggbert was thinking he'd found the perfect place, a potato plant happened to notice his crack. "Split!" the plant ordered.

Eggbert tried not to be discouraged. "Maybe I'll have better luck outdoors," he said to himself.

The only way down was to jump.

Luckily, Eggbert landed in a soft bed of flowers. He had never seen flowers before. But they smelled even better than butter and lettuce. Perhaps this is the perfect place for me, he thought.

A dab here, a splotch there. *Voilà!* Eggbert was covered with flowers.

But late that afternoon, an angry bee discovered that
you cannot get nectar from an egg. Again, Eggbert was
told to leave.

It was getting dark, and he still had not found a place to live. Just when he was about to give up all hope, a glimmer of something caught his eye.

"What beautiful little lights," Eggbert whispered. With all his might, and twice his usual care, he climbed up the fence. "Perfect," Eggbert said, when he was covered with stars.

But the next morning, when the night stars were gone, a cat discovered that Eggbert was just an egg with a cracked shell.

"Scramble," said the cat.

Eggbert took a hard fall on the sidewalk. Now he was more cracked than ever. As it started to rain, he began to sob. He realized that no matter how he painted himself, he could not hide who he was.

Finally the rain stopped, and the sun broke through a crack in the clouds. Eggbert began to notice something he had never noticed in his whole life:

The world was full of cracks—all sorts of wonderful cracks!

Maybe it's not such a bad thing to be slightly cracked, he thought.

From then on, Eggbert traveled around the world...

...making new friends and seeing famous cracked sights.

But he never forgot his friends back home in the fridge.
And he painted them beautiful postcards of his travels.

They were well and truly amazed. And they missed him, if the truth be told.

To this day Eggbert does not regret being cracked. In fact, he is even a little proud of it.